Maggie and Pie
and the Perfect Picnic

By Carolyn Cory Scoppettone
Art by Paula J. Becker

HIGHLIGHTS PRESS
Honesdale, Pennsylvania

Stories + Puzzles = Reading Success!

Dear Parents,

Highlights Puzzle Readers are an innovative approach to learning to read that combines puzzles and stories to build motivated, confident readers.

Developed in collaboration with reading experts, the stories and puzzles are seamlessly integrated so that readers are encouraged to read the story, solve the puzzles, and then read the story again. This helps increase vocabulary and reading fluency and creates a satisfying reading experience for any kind of learner. In addition, solving puzzles fosters important reading and learning skills such as:

- shape and letter recognition
- letter-sound relationships
- visual discrimination
- logic
- flexible thinking
- sequencing

With high-interest stories, humorous characters, and trademark puzzles, Highlights Puzzle Readers offer a winning combination for inspiring young learners to love reading.

This is Maggie.

This is Pie.

Maggie and Pie love to cook. But sometimes Maggie gets a little **mixed up**.

You can help by **using the clues** to find the supplies they need.

"The pineapple is in the pantry.
It is on the top shelf.
It is next to the bananas.
It is in a blue can with a yellow label.
Can you find it?" asks Pie.

Happy reading!

PICNIC TODAY!

The sun is high in the sky.

"Look!" says Maggie. "A plane!"

"There is a picnic today," says Pie.

"Can we go to the picnic?"
asks Maggie.

"Yes!" says Pie.
"We can bring fruit salad.
Here is a recipe."

"First, we need two bowls," says Pie.

"I can help," says Maggie.

"What is that for?" asks Pie.

"You said we need to bowl.

I got my lucky ball," says Maggie.

"Oh no," sighs Pie.

"We need two *mixing* bowls."

"The bowls are on the middle shelf.

They are both red.

One is the smallest bowl.

One is the biggest bowl.

Can you find them?" asks Pie.

"Here are the bowls," says Maggie.

"Thanks," says Pie.

"Now we need some strawberries."

"Here is the straw," says Maggie.

"But where are the straw's berries?"

"Oh no," sighs Pie.

"We need *strawberries*."

"The strawberries are on the top shelf.

They are in a pink box.

They are next to the eggs.

They are not next to the tomatoes.

Can you find them?" asks Pie.

"Here are the strawberries," says Maggie.

"Thanks," says Pie.

"Now we need some pineapples."

"Silly Pie," says Maggie.

"Pine trees don't have apples."

"Oh no," sighs Pie.

"The pineapple is in the pantry.

It is on the top shelf.

It is next to the bananas.

It is in a blue can with a yellow label.

Can you find it?" asks Pie.

"Here is the pineapple,"
says Maggie.

"Thanks," says Pie. "Now we need
to make the dressing."

"Okay!" says Maggie. "I am ready for the picnic."

"Oh no," sighs Pie. "Not dresses. We need a topping for the salad."

"We need plain yogurt," says Pie.

"I can get it!" says Maggie.

"What is that?" asks Pie.

"You asked for a plane,"
says Maggie.

"Oh no," sighs Pie. "Not an airplane.
Plain yogurt!"

"The plain yogurt is in the refrigerator.

It is in a white jar.

It is next to the oranges.

It is not next to the bread.

Can you find it?" asks Pie.

"Here is the plain yogurt," says Maggie.

"Thank you," says Pie.

"I will mix this with some honey."

"Our fruit salad is ready," says Pie.

"Can we go to the picnic now?"
asks Maggie.

"What time does the picnic start?

Look on the flyer," says Pie.

"Here is a flier," says Maggie.

"But it does not say the time."

"Oh no," sighs Pie.

"Look at the picnic flyer on the table."

"Why didn't you say so?"
asks Maggie.

"We are finally at the picnic!"
says Maggie.

"It is a very nice day," says Pie
This is the perfect picnic!"

"*Buzz, buzz, buzz!*" says Maggie.

"Why are you making that sound?"
asks Pie.

"It's not a picnic without a fly!"
says Maggie.

1-2-3 Fruit Salad

1. Prep.

ADULT: Before you begin, chop the nuts and cut the fruit.

Wash your hands or wings!

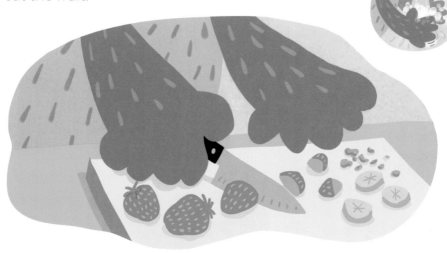

2. Combine.

In a small bowl, combine

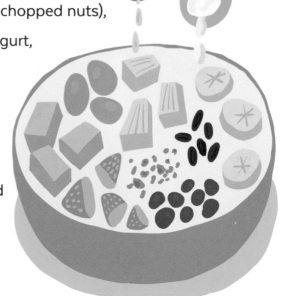

- **1** teaspoon honey,
- **2** teaspoons raisins (or chopped nuts),
- **3** tablespoons plain yogurt,
- **4** grapes,
- **5** bananas slices,
- **6** cantaloupe chunks,
- **7** pineapple chunks,
- **8** strawberry slices, and
- **9** blueberries.

3. Stir.

Stir **10** times.

What other fruits could you add to this salad?

For information about permission to reprint
selections from this book, please contact
permissions@highlights.com.

Published by Highlights Press
815 Church Street
Honesdale, Pennsylvania 18431
ISBN (paperback): 978-1-64472-697-6
ISBN (hardcover): 978-1-64472-698-3
ISBN (ebook): 978-1-64472-699-0

Library of Congress Control Number: 2021950409
Printed in Melrose Park, IL, USA
Mfg. 03/2022

First edition
Visit our website at Highlights.com.
10 9 8 7 6 5 4 3 2 1

For assistance in the preparation of this book,
the editors would like to thank Julie Tyson, MSEd
Reading, MSEd Administration K–12, Title 1 Reading
Specialist; and Gina Shaw.